MW00887347

ISBN: 9781717821621

ACKNOWLEDGMENTS

For all the wonderful dogs and pets in rescue shelters who are waiting patiently to live happily ever after in their forever homes with their forever humans, and for the efforts of all those human heroes who have dedicated their lives to loving and caring for these pets until they find their forever homes.

DEDICATION

To my FANmily who continue to inspire me daily with love and friendship, and who also encouraged me to write this book. To my friend and manager, Michael Yanni. And of course, to Dogbert and Tito who made this book possible.

"Are you ready, Tito? It's time to leave."

Dogbert the German shepherd was always ready to go anywhere with his human. He couldn't understand why his little brother, Tito the English Bull Dog, was still on his pillow.

Tito wasn't a little puppy anymore, but he was still young and new to their routines. This was their first hike of the spring season that year, and it was the first spring season Tito would remember.

"I'm coming. I'm coming, calm yourself," Tito said. He yanked his pillow from the chair to the floor, climbed back into bed, and tried to ignore Dogbert.

Dogbert's human rubbed the top of his head, which was something he did often, and said, "We're using the leashes today, guys. Don't look at me that way, Dogbert. I know you hate leashes. But Tito still isn't used to his leash yet and he needs the practice. It won't be forever. He'll get used to it sooner or later. Remember that he's a lot younger than you are, Dogbert."

Dogbert sent Tito a look and shook his head. "You heard him, pal, let's get moving." They didn't speak through words and sentences like humans. They spoke through their eyes and with the emotions they felt deep down inside...the magic of dog love.

Tito had moved to another part of the room by then. He was resting on the floor now. He yawned and said, "Okay. I'm ready."

A few minutes later, Dogbert nudged his little brother on the head with his paw and said, “Stick with me, buddy. I know you’ll get the hang of all this eventually. You’re still young. Rule number one: don’t be too eager. You have to let the humans think they are in charge. They like that.” He felt kind of bad for Tito, and also responsible. He still had so much to learn about life.

It wasn’t that long ago when Tito was just a chubby ball of white fluff who tended to waddle and wobble when he walked.

As they waited for their human to get the leashes ready, Tito looked up at Dogbert and spoke with a soft, high-pitched voice. "It's still dark outside. It's scary. I want to go back to bed. Who gets up this early?"

"Listen, buddy," Dogbert said. He looked forward to getting up early and going for these walks to see the sunrise over Runyon Canyon. "You'd better get used to it. When the mornings get warmer, this is how things are done around here."

"Where's he taking us?" Tito asked.

"It all depends," Dogbert said. "Sometimes it's around the neighborhood where we usually run into a mean old Squirrelbert who lives in the trees. The Squirrelberts are sneaky ones, and fast, too. And other times we go to a place called Runyon Canyon where there are a lot of other humans walking their dogs."

"What's a *Squirrelbert*?" Tito asked.

"It's like a rat with a big bushy tail," Dogbert said. "It's fast and knows how to run up a tree."

"Sounds scary," Tito said.

"They can be scary, but not as scary as the big kitty cat," Dogbert said. "She can be grouchy. All you have to do is smile at her and she'll let out the worst hissing sound you've ever heard. And don't try to sniff her tail whatever you do. You'll get your nose scratched. But you're lucky because I'm around. No one will mess with you as long as you're with me."

Then their human tugged on their leashes and said, "C'mon, guys, we don't want to miss the sunrise. I have a feeling it's going to be the best sunrise ever."

"He says that every morning," Dogbert said. "And you know, he's always right. It is always the best sunrise ever."

As Dogbert watched his little brother, Tito, wobble down the sidewalk, he knew he had to make sure Tito learned how to do things the right way.

"Why can't we sit up front with him?" Tito asked. Their human had just removed their leashes and closed the back door of the truck.

"I'm not sure," Dogbert said. "We always sit in the backseat and the humans always sit up front."

"But why? There must be a reason," Tito said.

Dogbert shook his head. Tito tended to ask too many questions. "Because it's the law. That's all you need to know. Now sit back and stop talking or you'll roll all over the place."

"Okay."

Not long after that, the truck came to a halt and their human climbed out so he could open the back door and put their leashes on again. "Are you guys ready? Here we go. It's a beautiful morning. It's the best morning ever."

"Where are we going now?" Tito asked. "I smell something good. Yum, I'm getting hungry."

"Just follow me, buddy," Dogbert said. The chubby little guy sure did have a good sense of smell, especially when it came to food. "Someone must have snacks. I think it's pizza."

"What are *snacks*?" Tito asked. "I know you told me but I forgot."

"Do you remember that time our human took us to the butcher shop and they let us taste a few things? Well, it's like that. Snacks are pieces of food they give you if you're good," Dogbert said. "Sometimes they call them treats. It could be anything from pizza to bacon. And pizza is one of the best snacks ever. But all snacks are good. I never had a snack I didn't like."

"Okay."

It was still dark outside, but there was a subtle glimmer on the horizon and it would be dawn soon. As they climbed the trail, they passed the yappy little girl dog who liked to bark at Dogbert for no reason whatsoever. Her human made no attempt to quiet her.

"What's wrong with her?" Tito asked. "Why does she bark at nothing?"

Dogbert shrugged and said, "The little ones like to be heard. It's all about them."

A few minutes after that, they passed the human who never put his dog on a leash, and if any dog ever needed to be on a leash it was him. He was a skinny, medium sized mixed breed who never stopped moving and bouncing around in all different directions.

And he listened to nothing his human told him to do.

The moment the nervous dog without the leash noticed Tito, he charged over to them on the trail and growled at Tito. It was a deep and scary growl and Tito took a few steps back.

So Dogbert walked up next to Tito and growled right back at the skinny dog and said, "Back off, Pal. This is my little brother and you're going to be dealing with me until he learns how to take care of himself."

A few other dogs came over to see what was happening, and the skinny dog stopped barking and stared up and down at Dogbert. When he saw in Dogbert's eyes that he wasn't fooling around, he turned all the way around and trained his gaze on a human walking a Chihuahua. This made Dogbert chuckle. Dogbert knew the Chihuahua, and he could be meaner than the kitty cat who lived next door.

When they reached a certain point in the trail that overlooked the hills, Dogbert's human pulled his phone out of his pocket and turned east toward the sunrise. While he clicked a photo so he could share it with all of his Internet friends throughout the world, Dogbert sat by his side and gazed at the sky. For some reason he couldn't understand, the sunrise always made him homesick for something he couldn't even describe.

"What are we doing and why did we stop?" Tito asked.

"Get over here and sit down next to me," Dogbert said. "We're looking at the sunrise. This is quiet time. No talking." He'd never met a dog who talked as much as Tito.

No two sunrises were ever the same. The one they watched that morning was more colorful than others, filled with hope and magic and all the awesomeness the universe contained. Tito wobbled over and sat right beside Dogbert in such a faithful, adorable way, Dogbert lifted his right front leg and rested his paw across Tito's back.

Dogbert had started doing this a few weeks earlier in the backyard on the grass. Whenever he put his paw on Tito's back it seemed to reassure him.

Their human was still holding his phone and taking photos of the sunrise. When he glanced down and saw Dogbert's arm around Tito, he snapped a photo and said, "You guys are too much. Good boy, Dogbert. You take care of him. He needs all the help he can get." Then he laughed and took a few more photos of them to share with his Internet friends before they started moving again.

When they finally reached Dogbert's favorite place on the entire trail, their human stopped and said, "I don't see any around here today, Dogbert."

"What's he talking about? What's he looking for?" Tito asked.

Dogbert looked out over a large group of rocks. The poor thing didn't remember anything Dogbert had told him. "He's talking about sticks. I thought I already told you about this. Sticks are very important," Dogbert said. "You have to have a good stick on a hike, and the bigger the better."

Tito tilted his head to the side. "Why?"

"It's complicated," Dogbert said. He was starting to think that Tito thought his name was Googlebert instead of Dogbert.

Then Dogbert spotted a stick that his human had missed. It was poking up from behind a large rock in the distance. He began jumping around in a playful way, as if trying to head in that direction so his human would unhook him from the leash.

"What are you doing?" Tito asked. "You look silly."

"Just pay attention and learn."

Their human was quick to sense Dogbert's excitement. "Do you see one, Dogbert?"

Dogbert let out a soft bark and rubbed his head against his human's leg. The stick he spotted reminded him of one he'd picked up last year on the trails.

His human seemed to understand and he reached down to unhook the leash from his collar. "Go get it, Dogbert. Good boy. You get that stick."

Tito stood up taller. "Why can't I come, too? I can help."

As Dogbert took off toward the rock, he sent Tito a backward glance and said, "Just wait here for me. You're not ready yet. This is going to be the biggest stick I've ever had."

The stick turned out to be so long and so thick it reminded Dogbert of a massive branch that fell across a fence once in his neighborhood.

However, it wasn't quite as huge as that branch and he finally took hold of it, pulled it out from behind the rock, and turned so he could drag it back to his human. This was his favorite part of finding a good stick: bringing it back so his human could tell him how fantastic it was.

He was certain this stick would garner him more praise than usual. The sheer length alone made it worth his while. It had to be the biggest most awesome stick he'd ever found. It was so long and so heavy he could only lift one half with his mouth and drag the other half back to the trail.

Then something unusual happened. When he reached the trail he found his human talking to another human. Seeing them talk reminded Dogbert of another hike when he'd found a much smaller stick in the grass.

His human was talking to the pretty young woman with the soft voice and blond hair. She smelled like flowers and pizza and donuts and reminded Dogbert of the best sunrises ever. Best of all, she always reached down to pet his head so gently it was almost as good as snacks.

Only this time the pretty woman was all alone. She usually hiked the trail with her dog, an older female German shepherd they called Posh who had been having trouble with her hind legs recently. Last time Dogbert had seen Posh, she told him, "It's been hard. It's like I can't get my back legs to move the way I want them to move. My human had to put rugs in the house so I can get up. I can't even think about stairs. I'm trying so hard to get better."

On that afternoon Dogbert gave her his small stick and said, "That's a shame, Posh. I hope it gets better." He could sense something about her that was not possible to explain. It came to him through her scent and by the gentle look in her eyes. There was something wrong with her and he knew there was nothing he could do to make it better.

Now Dogbert's human was so lost in conversation with the young woman he didn't even notice the fantastic, wondrous stick Dogbert was carrying. They were talking about something called Degenerative Myelopathy, which they referred to as DM for short, and how it could hurt dogs.

The pretty woman said DM was a lot like something humans get called MS. Dogbert's ears went up when she told his human about how the veterinarian was treating her dog's DM. The veterinarian's office was not Dogbert's favorite place to go in the world. They had cold floors, they made him stand on something called a scale, and the veterinarian told his human no more snacks.

But even worse than that, most of the time they stuck his butt with something sharp and pointy that made his skin hurt for a second or two.

Their human might have been talking too much to notice the huge stick, but Tito noticed it and he got that glorious, dreamy look in his eyes. For a moment, he got so excited he rolled over on his back in a small grassy area and almost rolled on top of Dogbert.

Dogbert had seen that look before with other dogs. It was all about the stick, and this stick was so epic and so fantastically awesome it simply could not be ignored by any dog on the planet.

"That's the best stick ever," Tito said, still on his back. "Can I hold it? Please, Dogbert. Let me hold it."

Dogbert said, “If you think you can, be my guest. But I think it’s a little too big for you.” This reminded Dogbert of the time Tito found a pine cone on the street where they lived. At the time, he couldn’t wait to pick up the pine cone, but he didn’t like the way it tasted.

Of course Tito didn’t realize he wasn’t as big as Dogbert and he tried to wrap his flat little English bulldog jaw around the huge stick.

When Tito finally realized he couldn't lift the stick, he ran behind an old fence and Dogbert followed him to make sure he wouldn't get into trouble.

Their human stopped talking to the pretty woman and laughed at the way they were leaning on the fence. "What's wrong, Teets? Is that stick too big for you? We'll have to find you a smaller one."

Tito flung a look at Dogbert. "Why did he call me *Teets*? I thought my name was Tito."

"It's a nickname," Dogbert said. In all fairness to Tito, it was the first time their human called him Teets. "Humans love nicknames. You'll get used to it."

The pretty woman who smelled like flowers and pizza and donuts crouched down to rub the top of Tito's head gently. "You sweet little fat thing. I hope you can meet my baby soon. She's not feeling well today so I had to leave her home."

There was an unmistakable sadness in her voice that tugged at Dogbert's heart so hard he felt a sting in his eye and didn't know how to process it.

Tito rolled over on his back again so she could rub his belly. Tito loved his belly rubs. If he thought a human would rub his belly, he would roll over anywhere, from the rug on their living room floor to the sandy trails of Runyon.

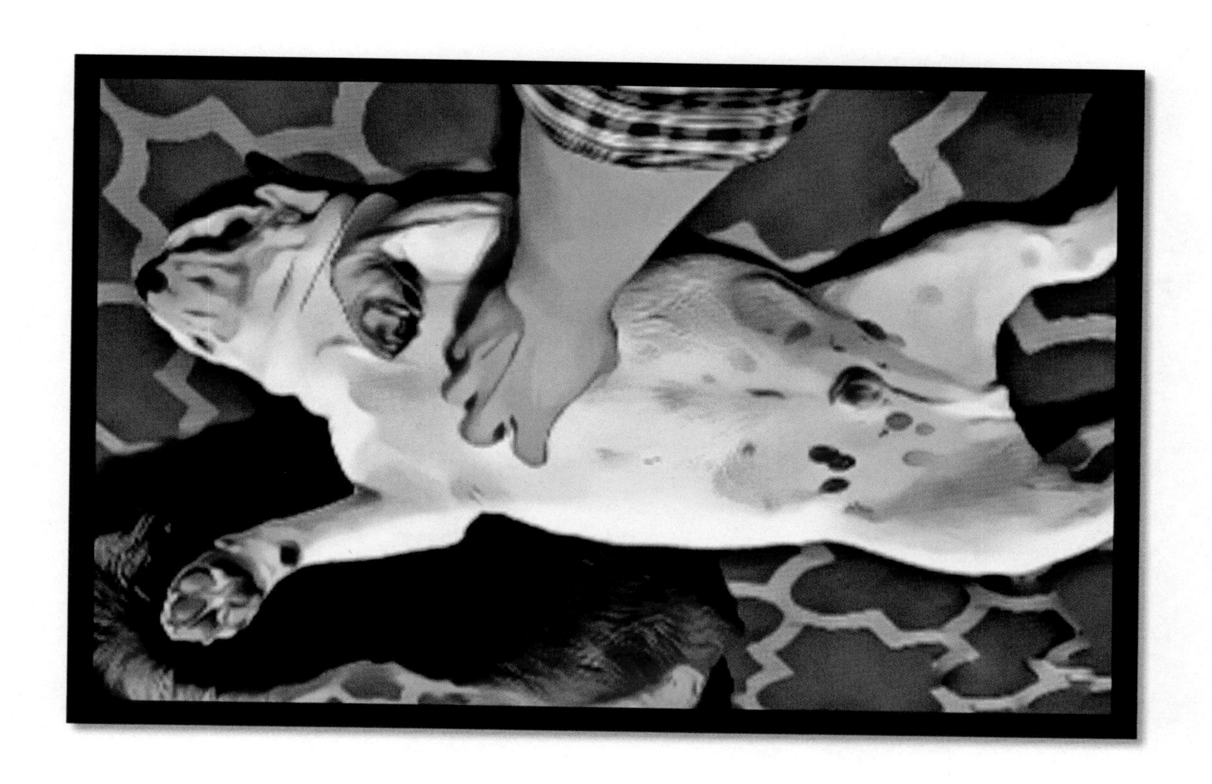

And that's when Dogbert knew the lady had one of the great gifts of the universe. She could communicate with animals without speaking a single word and know exactly what they were feeling. But more than that, it came to her like it comes to most people like her, so easily and so naturally she didn't even realize she had the gift.

Dogbert also noticed a sadness in her eyes that made him want to run up and lick her face. He would have done that, too, if his human hadn't said, "Okay, guys. Time to go home now. Everybody is getting a bath today. Tito stinks from our trip to the dog park yesterday."

Tito looked up at Dogbert. "What's a bath?"

Dogbert didn't have the heart to tell him. This was something they did on warmer days. He had this feeling Tito was the type who would run for cover the minute he saw the tub and the garden hose coming out.

Dogbert rested his arm on Tito's back. "You'll see what a bath is in good time. It's what they do to you when you roll around in the dirt like you did yesterday at the dog park."

Then Dogbert picked up his stick and tried to carry it all the way back to where they'd left the truck. He knew he wouldn't get very far, though, and that didn't really bother him all that much. There was always another stick that was bigger, better and way more awesome than the one before it.

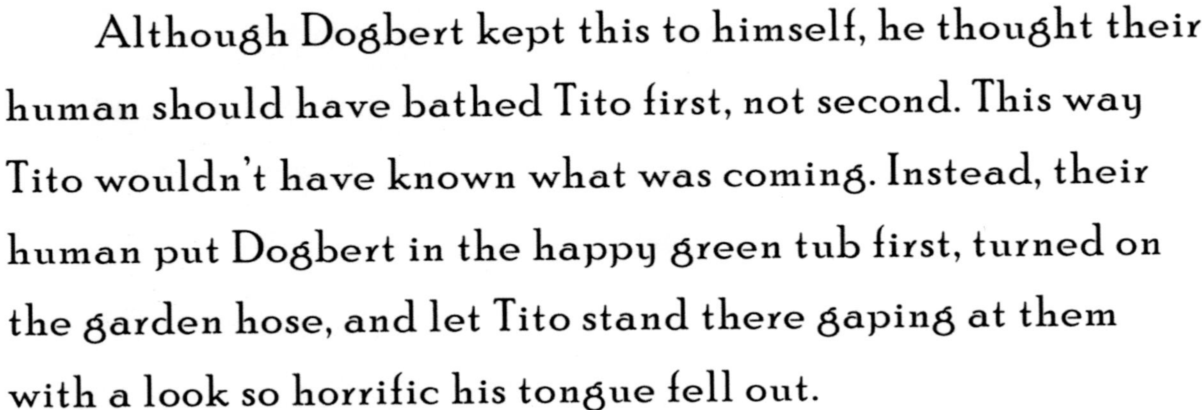

Although Dogbert kept this to himself, he thought their human should have bathed Tito first, not second. This way Tito wouldn't have known what was coming. Instead, their human put Dogbert in the happy green tub first, turned on the garden hose, and let Tito stand there gaping at them with a look so horrific his tongue fell out.

The poor kid, he actually started to shake. By the time Dogbert's bath was over and he shook the excess bath water all over the patio, Tito took off so fast their human almost tripped over a potted palm tree in his bare feet trying to catch him. Tito might have been small, but you should have seen that chubby little bulldog run.

While their human carried Tito back to the tub, Dogbert moved into the sunlight to dry off and said, "Don't fight it, buddy. You don't get a choice. They like us clean around here, and seriously, dude, you do stink."

"I think I smell just fine," Tito said. "I like the way I smell. I don't want to do this."

Dogbert laughed and said, "Too bad, pal."

Their human put a funny blue cap on Tito's head so he wouldn't get water in his ears, but Tito never stopped moving once during the bath. And when he finally did get out of the tub the first thing he did was fall down on the dusty patio floor and roll around again.

"Oh, dude," Dogbert said. "You've got this all wrong. You're going to get dirty all over again and that just means another bath."

Tito continued to roll around from side to side. "I don't care."

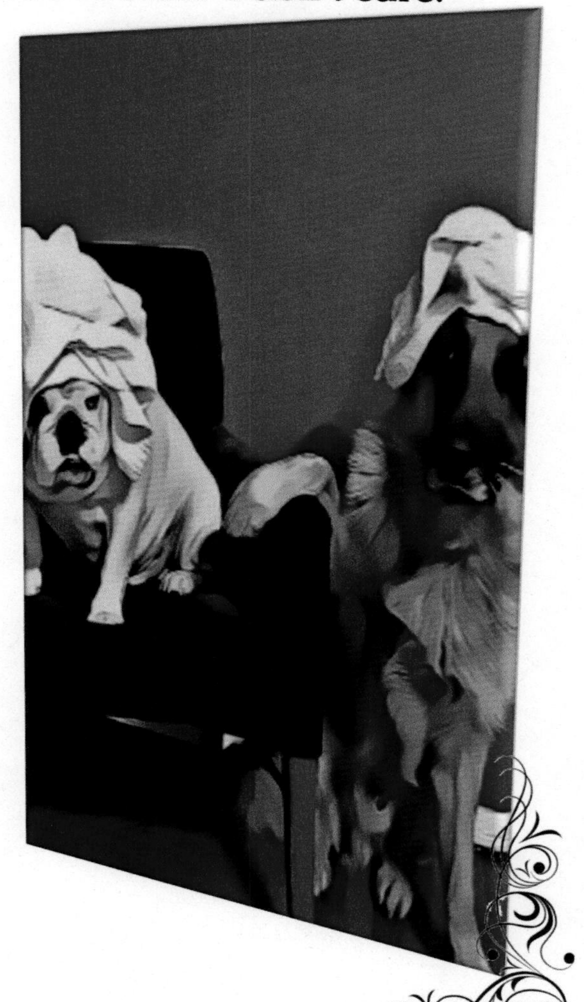

Dogbert remembered his very first bath and he'd felt the same exact way. "The good news is that we don't have to do this every day."

Their human turned off the garden hose and said, "I'll be right back, Dogbert and Tito."

Dogbert barked. "Oh, you'll like this. He's going to get snacks. That's the only good thing about getting a bath. You always get a snack afterward, and it's usually a good one."

On that afternoon, their human gave them a snack of special healthy doggie pizza; the really good crispy kind Dogbert liked the most. And for dinner that night Tito got some kind of healthy food their veterinarian had recommended and Dogbert got a nice big raw chicken breast with all the bones. This was one of Dogbert's favorite meals and always one worth waiting for. He enjoyed it so much he carried the chicken breast over to his doggie bed, turned his back on everyone, and ate it in his own little corner of the house so no one could bother him.

Tito looked up from his bowl and asked, "Hey, I want what you have. How come you get that and I get this other stuff."

"You're too little for this," Dogbert said. He hated talking with his mouth full. "Now finish your own dinner and leave me alone."

"That's not fair."

Dogbert didn't reply. He wouldn't have wanted to watch another dog eat a nice big juicy raw chicken breast with all the bones while he had to sit there with a bowl of mushy food either.

After dinner, their human had a few friends come over and everyone sat outside around a fire pit listening to music and talking. They liked to eat, too. Dogbert always enjoyed nights like this the most because his human had some really cool friends who gave good snacks when no one was looking. Dogbert looked forward to those nights the most, especially when they dropped cheese on the floor and never even knew it.

On that particular night, while one friend was telling a story about something that had happened to him earlier that day and everyone else was laughing, Dogbert's old friend Hawkbert came back for a visit. He hadn't seen Hawkbert for a while and he'd been thinking about him.

"It's Hawkbert," Dogbert said.

Tito looked up. "Who's *Hawkbert?*"

"Only the coolest hawk ever."

The first time they'd all met Hawkbert he'd landed on their patio with a wing injury. That had been at least three years ago. It was in June, on a clear night that was as warm as it was still. They'd been sitting around just as they were that night, when all of a sudden the most elegant hawk swooped down from the sky and landed on one of the patio chairs.

No one knew what to do at first. Of course Dogbert knew the hawk had been injured and that he needed help. The hawk told him but there was no way Dogbert could explain that to the humans in detail. Thankfully, Dogbert's human figured it out and he phoned one of those wild animal rescue places. A nice young woman came, gently put the hawk into a cage, and carted him off to some kind of bird hospital where they could take good care of him. Hawkbert eventually recovered and the nice lady from animal rescue set him free again. And from that day on, Hawkbert returned to see Dogbert every once in a while to thank him for what they'd done.

When Dogbert saw Hawkbert gazing down on them that night, he sat up and started barking. His human pointed and said, "Look, there's Hawkbert. He came back for a visit."

The human's friends didn't think it was the same hawk and they laughed and made jokes about it. They went back to telling their stories and eating their snacks, and Dogbert looked up at Hawkbert and said, "Where have you been?"

"I've been around," Hawkbert said. "You know how it is."

Tito moved closer to Dogbert's pillow. "Does he eat English bulldogs? He looks mean."

Hawkbert and Dogbert laughed, and then Hawkbert said, "Calm down, little guy. I don't eat dogs. You guys are my friends and I only came to give you a message."

Dogbert moved closer to the house. "What kind of message?"

"There's a German shepherd named Posh who says you know her," Hawkbert said. "She wanted me to tell you that she's not doing well, but she loves you guys and just wants you to know that."

"What else did she say?" Dogbert asked. Hawkbert kept moving around and they had to follow him to a grassy area.

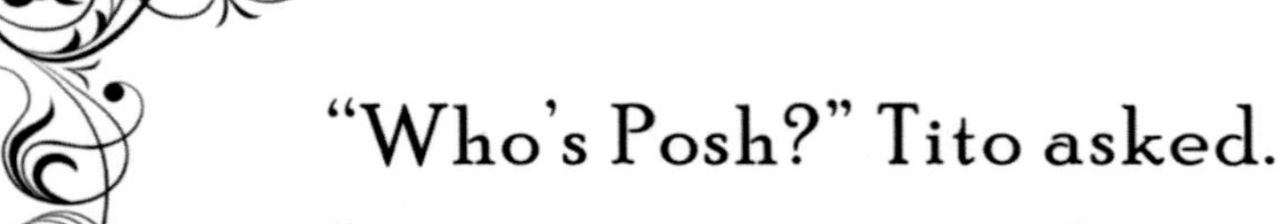

“Who’s Posh?” Tito asked.

“Pay attention, Tito,” Dogbert said. “Posh is a dog I know, and she belongs to the human we met today during the hike. The nice lady who smells like flowers and pizza and donuts.”

“Oh yeah,” Tito said. “She rubbed my belly. I like her.”

“Posh didn’t say anything else,” said Hawkbert. “All she said is that she loves you and she wanted you to know that.”

This didn’t sound good at all. It gave Dogbert a bad feeling. “Tell her the same goes for us,” Dogbert said.

Hawkbert nodded, and then he spread his wings and took off into the sky. He never stayed for long during his visits and by that time the humans didn’t realize he’d left.

Dogbert looked down at Tito and said, “I sure wish there was something we could do for Posh. She’s one of the good ones.”

Tito said, "Maybe the magic stick can help."

"What magic stick? What are you talking about now?"

"The one the old rabbit told me about."

"You're not making sense, Tito. What old rabbit told you about a magic stick?"

"There's this rabbit that lives over by the fence," Tito said. "I saw him this afternoon when I ran away from the bath tub. The rabbit told me the magic stick can do a lot of things that humans don't understand. Maybe it can help Posh feel better."

Dogbert had heard stories like this before, but he'd never actually come across anything real. The rabbits were considered the most spiritual of all the wild animals and they knew certain secrets of the universe no one else knew. Once in a while they would share one of their secrets.

"Do you know where this magic stick is?" Dogbert asked.

Tito nodded. "In that place with the plants and bushes."

"Take me over there and show me."

"Follow me."

They searched the shrubs and plants where Tito had hidden from his bath earlier that day. They found a few interesting sticks and Dogbert put his arm on Tito. "Well, which one is the magic stick?"

Tito looked at him and his ears went back. "I'm not sure. I can't remember."

"Well that's not going to help Posh," Dogbert said. He couldn't get mad at him because he was so young. What did he know about magic sticks?

"Sorry, Dogbert," Tito said. "I'll try harder to remember."

Then, out of nowhere came a deep, throaty voice. "It's the stick over there, the one next to the rock that looks like a watermelon."

Dogbert looked up at a cluster of flowers near a black iron fence and saw an old gray rabbit hiding in between the wall and a shrub. From what he'd heard, the older rabbits knew more than any other creature in the universe. They possessed gifts that went far beyond wisdom and knowledge. They knew secrets of the old days and they didn't share them often with anyone.

But Dogbert wasn't a fool. "Who are you?" Dogbert asked. "And why should we trust you?"

"It doesn't matter who I am, or whether or not you trust me," the rabbit said. "I'm nothing to you. I'm only letting you know there's a magic stick that will give your friend some relief. It won't cure what she has, but it will give her more time and she won't suffer. If you don't want to listen to me, that's your choice. I'm only sharing what I know out of the kindness of my tired old heart."

Dogbert nodded toward the rock that resembled a watermelon and said, "That's the stick, the small one?" He'd seen better sticks on his worst day at Runyon Canyon. It wasn't even as long as Tito, and there were no interesting swirls or twists or turns. The only thing he noticed that was different about it was that it had a slight glow. Not an obvious glow, and no human would ever notice it.

"Yes," the rabbit said, "that's the stick."

Dogbert stared at the stick for a moment, and then he glanced back to ask the rabbit another question. But the rabbit was gone by then, as if it had melted into the bushes. Dogbert looked at Tito and asked, "Where did the rabbit go?"

Tito gulped and said, "How should I know? I was looking at the magic stick."

Dogbert walked over to the stick with the glow and said, "We have to get this stick to Posh as soon as we can. There's not a moment to waste. I'm just not sure how we're going to do that, is all."

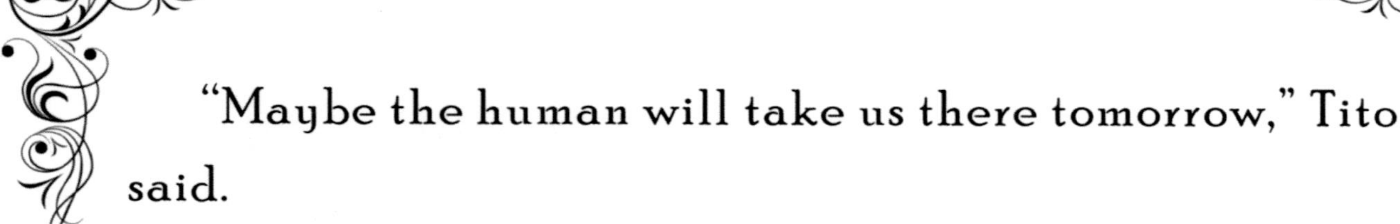

"Maybe the human will take us there tomorrow," Tito said.

"Why would he do that?" Dogbert knew the human had a morning routine, especially in the springtime when all the flowers bloomed.

"While you were eating that big chicken breast with all those delicious bones, I heard the human talking to that thing he takes pictures of the sunrise with," Tito said. "He told the lady who smells like flowers he would stop by her house with something for Posh. The human is going to drop it off tomorrow morning on his way to that canyon place. It's something to put in Posh's food that might help her feel better."

Dogbert rarely missed anything that went on around that house. He must have been too busy enjoying the raw chicken breast earlier. "You know, kid, you're pretty good. I have to admit that I was worried about you in the beginning. Now let's get the magic stick inside, put it in a safe place, and get it to Posh tomorrow morning on our way to the canyon."

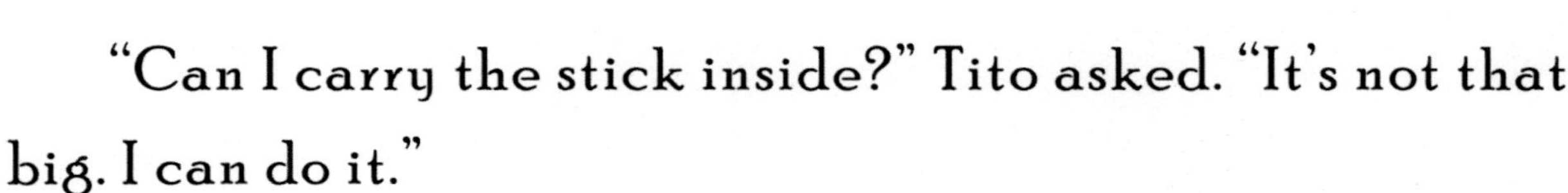

"Can I carry the stick inside?" Tito asked. "It's not that big. I can do it."

Dogbert put his arm around him and said, "Sure you can, kid. This one is all yours."

Tito carried the stick into the house and Dogbert followed through the doggie door their human had installed for them. They set the stick down near Dogbert's pillow and then faced each other. Dogbert gave Tito a stern look and said, "We have to make sure nothing happens to that stick between now and tomorrow morning. It's very important it remains safe here in this spot."

Tito nodded. "Okay."

The following morning they left the house later than usual. When their human opened the back door of the truck to help them inside he noticed that Dogbert was carrying a small stick.

"What's that, Dogbert? Are you bringing your own stick along this morning?"

Dogbert jumped into the truck and settled into the backseat with the stick between his teeth. He looked at the human and made a soft noise. He knew he couldn't explain why he was carrying the stick in detail, but he also knew how to show the human he wanted to bring the stick along.

Tito had to be picked up because he was too small to climb in on his own. He was in a grumpy mood that morning because he didn't like getting up early. "I thought I was going to carry the stick. And I want to sit on his lap while he's driving."

"I'm carrying the stick this morning because it's too important," Dogbert said. He still wasn't even sure there was any magic in the stick. For all he knew the old rabbit could have been completely unhinged, or a blatant liar.

Before he closed the back door, their human reached inside and gave them each a hug. "You must really like that stick. I've never seen you hold onto a stick that long before."

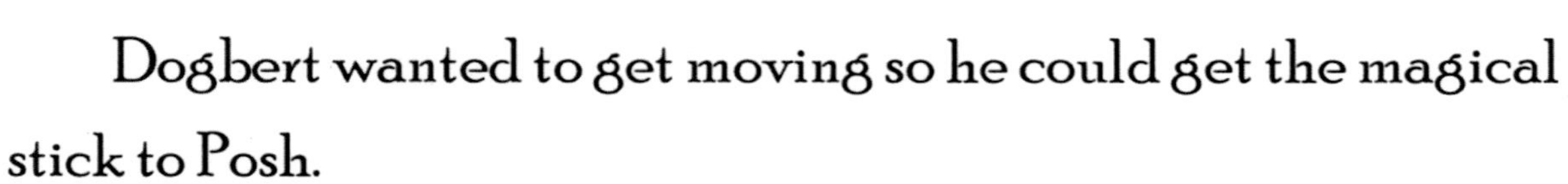

Dogbert wanted to get moving so he could get the magical stick to Posh.

The only thing that seemed to cheer Tito up that morning was resting his head on their human's shoulder.

A few minutes later, Tito asked, "Are we almost there yet?"

Dogbert looked out the window and said, "Yes, we're almost there."

They eventually pulled up to a small house with a white picket fence and their human turned off the truck. Dogbert noticed there was one of those really excellent trees out front, the kind their human liked to climb sometimes on their own street back home.

Their human opened the truck's windows and said, "You guys wait here. I'll be right back. I just have to drop this off for Posh. It's a vitamin that might make her feel better."

Dogbert had to go in there with him. He had to get that magic stick to Posh. So he started leaping around in the backseat, poking Tito with his snout.

Even though Tito was still as grumpy as he had been when they left the house, Dogbert told Tito to bark because he couldn't bark with a stick in his mouth. And for once in his life Tito listened to him without asking any questions.

"Why are you two jumping around and barking like that?" their human asked. "Do you want to come inside with me? Why not? I don't think Posh's mom will mind. She loves you guys."

After he hooked them both to their leashes, their human noticed the stick Dogbert was still carrying and said, "You can bring your stick inside, buddy."

Posh's mom, the nice lady who smelled like flowers, must have seen the truck pull up and stop out front. She was waiting for them on a bright, cheerful front porch lined with terra cotta containers of all different sizes that were filled with flowers of every color in the rainbow. Dogbert could feel the love in this house before he even walked up the front steps.

“I see you brought some friends along,” the nice lady said.

“These two wanted to come say hello to Posh,” their human said. “I hope that’s okay.”

“Of course it’s okay,” she said.

As she opened the front door, their human unfastened the leashes and said, “There you go.”

They ran up the steps and into the house to look for Posh. Dogbert led the way. The inside of the house smelled even better than it looked. He detected bacon, chicken, and pizza.

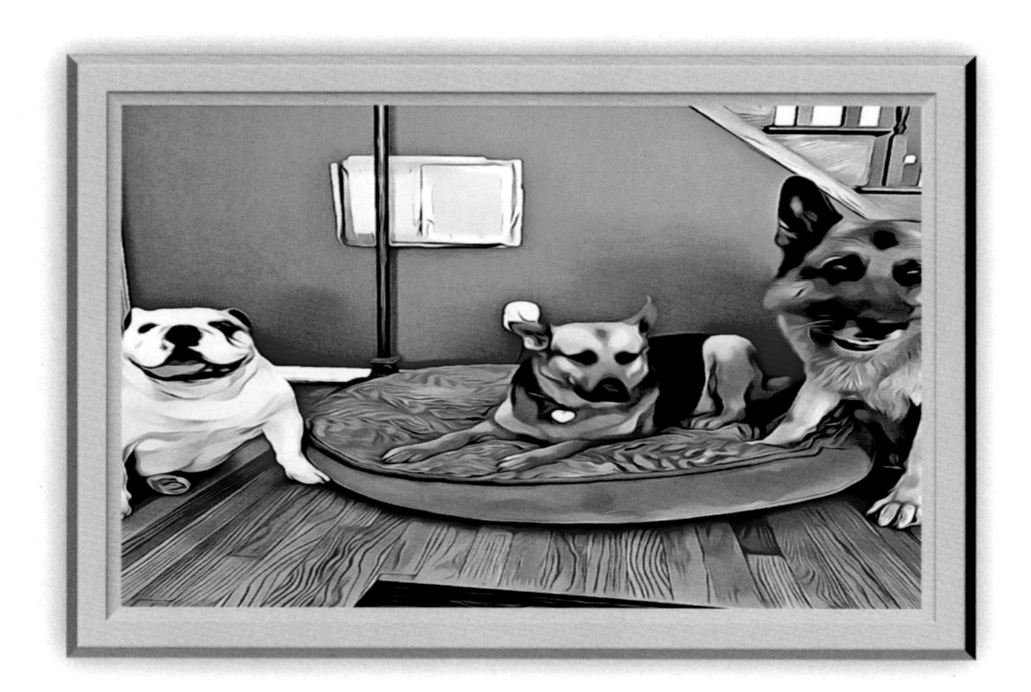

Dogbert still had the stick between his teeth inside the house. His human found that so amusing he said, "I think Dogbert is bringing a present to Posh."

The nice lady sighed. "I hope it will cheer her up. All she does is sleep now."

While the humans went into the kitchen, Dogbert and Tito rushed to the living room where they found Posh resting comfortably on a fluffy cushion.

Posh was surprised to see them. She lifted her head fast and said, "Hi, Dogbert, I'm sorry I can't get up. Hi Tito."

They walked over to her and Tito tried to sniff her tail.

"You have to excuse Tito," Dogbert said. "He doesn't know anything yet." He flung Tito a look. "Stop that, Tito."

Posh laughed. "He's okay. He's adorable."

She looked so helpless on the pillow it tugged at Dogbert's heart. "Are you in pain?"

"No," she said. "There's no pain with what I have. I have trouble moving my legs. It's hard to explain. My human understands it all better than I do. I just wish I had a little more time to do the normal things that I miss doing, all the things I took for granted all my life. That's all I'm asking for. I promise I would cherish every moment."

"We brought you something," Tito said. "It's the most magical awesomest stick ever."

"It's what?" she asked.

"The magic stick is supposed to be a gift of the universe," Dogbert said. "A wise old rabbit told us about it, and we figured it couldn't hurt. The old rabbit said it wouldn't cure you, but it would give you more time and make you a little better. That's all I know."

"What do I do with it?" Posh asked.

"I guess you should pick it up and see what happens," Dogbert said. He wasn't totally sure himself. The old rabbit had disappeared so quickly he didn't have time to ask.

"Yes, pick it up," Tito said. He'd gone under a table, as if worried about what might happen. "It's magic. You'll see."

Dogbert and Posh exchanged a long glance, and then Posh reached for the stick with her snout. While Tito watched closely, she picked the magic stick up slowly and remained there staring at Dogbert, waiting to see what might happen next.

Nothing out of the ordinary happened, at least not at first. There were no fireworks, bolts of lightning, or pounds of thunder. The skies didn't light up and celestial choirs didn't start singing. For a moment, Dogbert's heart sank because he didn't think anything would happen at all.

And then Posh set the stick down on the pillow and Dogbert watched her back legs move around.

He was too stunned to move.

"Look," Tito said. "She's moving. The magic stick worked. I knew it would work."

A moment after that, Posh stood up on her own and said, "Look at me. I'm standing for the first time in a week. I think I can even walk."

At the exact moment Posh took a step forward from her cushion, their humans walked into the living room and stopped short in their tracks.

The nice lady covered her mouth with her hands and gasped.

Their human pressed his palm to his throat and said, "She's walking."

"I know. I don't understand it," the nice lady said. "The vet told me it wasn't going to get any better."

"Maybe her medications are working now," their human said.

"I guess they are," the lady said, and then she ran over to Posh, went down on her knees, and hugged her until they both had tears running down their faces.

While the lady hugged Posh, their human did the same to them. And when their human gave Tito a hug, Dogbert rested his paw on his human's shoulder to show him how thankful he was, too.

While the humans talked more about medications, Posh walked back to her pillow to rest. "How long will this last?"

"I don't know," Dogbert said. "How do you feel?"

Posh moved her back legs a few times. "I feel fine," she said. "I'm not as fast as I used to be, but I can move and stand and do all the things I need to do. I have more time now, and I promise you I will not waste a second of it."

Tito had been watching and listening to everything. "The rabbit told me there are all kinds of magical secrets in the universe no one knows about. This is only one of them. He said there are so many you can't even count them. The secret is believing. He told me if you don't believe in something special, nothing special will ever happen to you."

Dogbert put his arm around Tito and said, "I'll see if I can find out more, Posh. If I do, I'll tell Hawkbert and he can give you the message. For now just enjoy being able to walk again."

Then their human called their names and said, "C'mon, it's time to go outside. We have to hit the trails before it gets too late."

Tito didn't seem grumpy anymore either. He was playing with one of Posh's black rubber toys and didn't want to let go.

"C'mon, Tito," their human said.

On the way outside, as they headed back to the truck, Tito started tugging on their human's shoe, which was something he tended to do whenever they least expected it. Their human seemed to find it amusing and he encouraged it, but Dogbert found it irritating and said, "Tito, knock that off. When we get outside I have something special to show you."

Tito stopped chewing their human's foot and looked up. "Is it another stick?"

Dogbert shook his head. "No. It's even better than a stick."

"Better than a stick? What could be better than a stick?"

Dogbert nodded. "Follow me, bud. It's a surprise. You're going to love this."

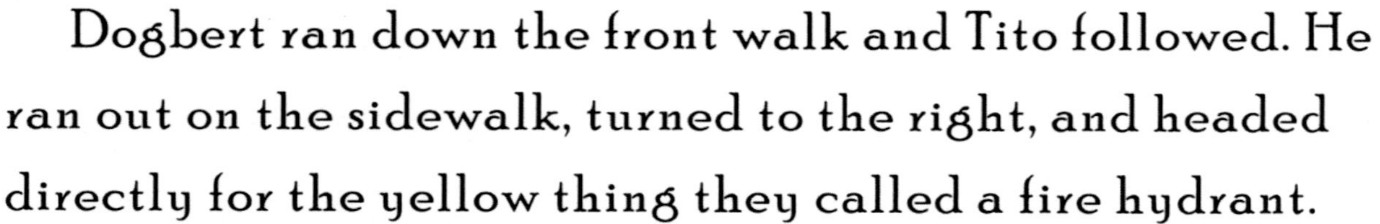

Dogbert ran down the front walk and Tito followed. He ran out on the sidewalk, turned to the right, and headed directly for the yellow thing they called a fire hydrant.

As Dogbert turned to watch Tito run toward him, he grew filled with hope for the future. The world was such a magical place. He would teach Tito everything he had to know, and show him how to do things the right way. And Dogbert would look for the rabbit in the shrubs again, and try to find out more secrets of the universe that might help other dogs like Posh get relief from their afflictions and illnesses.

A second or two later, his human called him by his name and promised there would be an extra special treat for both of them after their morning hike.

Dogbert poked Tito with his snout, and said, "Are you ready, Tito? It's time to leave."

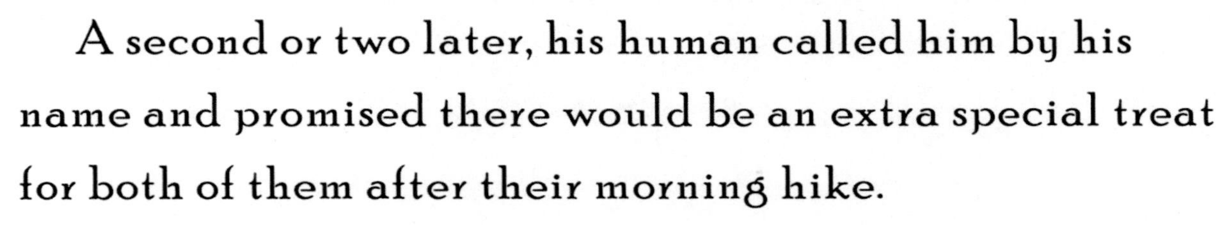

About the Author

Trevor Donovan was born in Mammoth Lakes, California. Trevor grew up skiing and snowboarding and, during his teens, was on the US teen ski team. Trevor is a true renaissance man, aside from being proficient at most sports, he can play guitar, sing, and has a bachelors degree in graphic design. Trevor is currently an ambassador for Habitat for Humanity, and an active volunteer and ambassador with Robert F. Kennedy Center for Justice & Human Rights.

Trevor currently resides in both Mammoth and Los Angeles. When not working, Trevor enjoys spending quality time with his family.

Made in the USA
Lexington, KY
18 September 2018